P9-CLB-476

**BEFORE I MET YOU,
I DREAMED OF YOU.
THIS IS THE STORY OF
HOW WE FIRST MET.**

ABOUT THIS BOOK

The illustrations for this book were done in Photoshop. This book was edited by Liz Kossnar and designed by Sasha Illingworth. The production was supervised by Nyamekye Waliyaya, and the production editor was Jen Graham. The text was set in Adobe Garamond Pro, and the display type is Bobby Jones.

Copyright © 2022 by Robin Arzón • Illustrations by Addy Rivera Sonda • Cover illustration by Addy Rivera Sonda • Cover design by Sasha Illingworth • Cover copyright © 2022 by Hachette Book Group, Inc. • Hachette Book Group supports the right to free expression and the value of copyright. The purpose of copyright is to encourage writers and artists to produce the creative works that enrich our culture. • The scanning, uploading, and distribution of this book without permission is a theft of the author's intellectual property. If you would like permission to use material from the book (other than for review purposes), please contact permissions@hbgusa.com. Thank you for your support of the author's rights. • Little, Brown and Company • Hachette Book Group

1290 Avenue of the Americas, New York, NY 10104 • Visit us at LBYR.com • First Edition: January 2022 • Little, Brown and Company is a division of Hachette Book Group, Inc. • The Little, Brown name and logo are trademarks of Hachette Book Group, Inc. • The publisher is not responsible for websites (or their content) that are not owned by the publisher. • Library of Congress Cataloging-in-Publication Data • Names: Arzón, Robin, author. | Sonda, Addy Rivera, illustrator. Title: Strong mama / by Robin Arzón ; illustrated by Addy Rivera Sonda. • Description: New York : Little, Brown and Company, [2022] | Audience: Ages 4–8 | Summary: "Mama and baby make a healthy and powerful team in this journey through pregnancy, fitness, and birth." —Provided by publisher. • Identifiers: LCCN 2021021192 | ISBN 9780316299947 (hardcover) | ISBN 9780316300049 (ebook) • Subjects: LCSH: Mother and infant—Juvenile literature. | Physical fitness for pregnant women—Juvenile literature. | Mothers—Health and hygiene—Juvenile literature. • Classification: LCC HQ755.84 .A79 2022 | DDC 306.874/3—dc23 LC record available at https://lccn.loc.gov/2021021192 • ISBNs: 978-0-316-29994-7 (hardcover), 978-0-316-30004-9 (ebook), 978-0-316-40067-1 (ebook), 978-0-316-40087-9 (ebook) • PRINTED IN THE UNITED STATES OF AMERICA • PHX • 10 9 8 7 6 5 4 3 2

ROBIN ARZÓN
STRONG MAMA

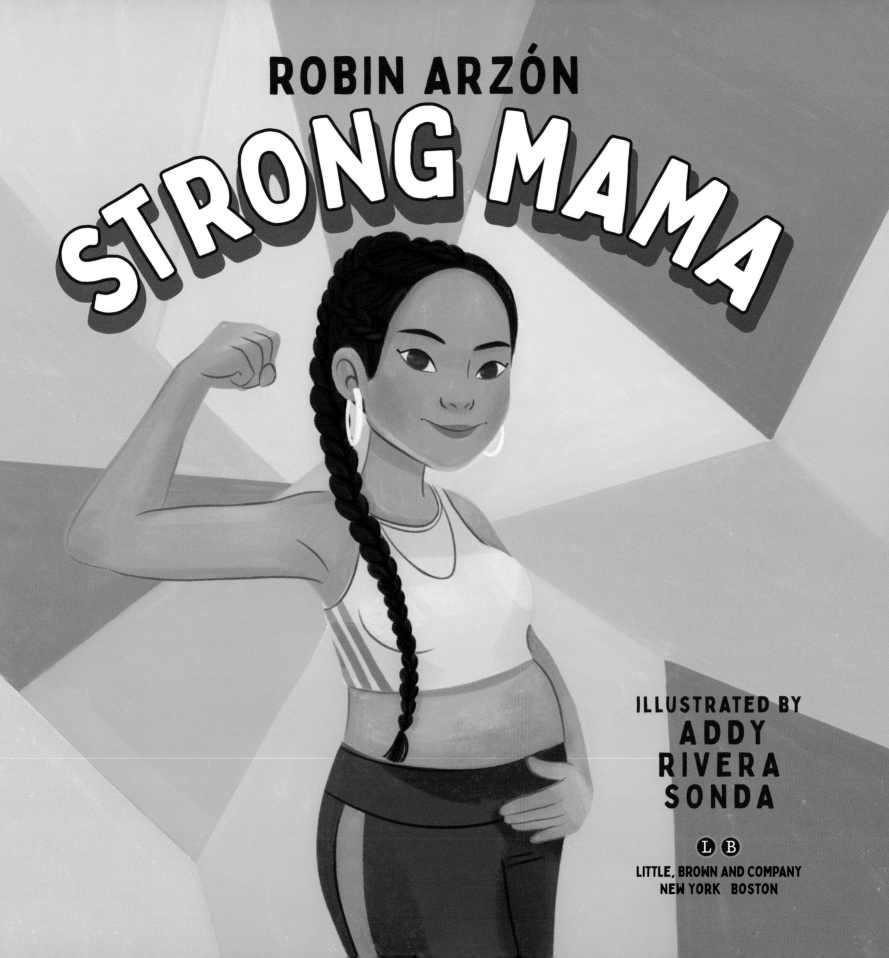

ILLUSTRATED BY
ADDY
RIVERA
SONDA

L B

LITTLE, BROWN AND COMPANY
NEW YORK   BOSTON

Your mama is an athlete. I've run thousands of miles and lifted hundreds of pounds to write an epic story painted in sweat. One that now includes you.

Growing you in my belly was hard work, but we
did it together. We became training partners.

We called you Pequeño. Little one. You are small,
but your legacy is a powerful one. Muy fuerte!

Your dad, abuela, abuelo, tías, tíos, and primos all loved you before they even met you. They were our cheerleaders, fueling us with love.

When I announced, "I'm pregnant!" they
cheered so loudly. You're our greatest triumph.

During your early visits to the doctor, we listened with special headphones. For the first time, I had two hearts in my body.

We went running over bridges, along the water, and
in the park to help our hearts beat stronger together.

We lifted weights to grow our muscles.

We prepared for victory as a team.

Little by little, week by week, our bond was growing, just like you were in Mommy's belly. And just like the number of fans cheering us on the Peloton leaderboard.

To keep us energized, Daddy made us yummy, nourishing foods, and we had kitchen dance parties. I taught you how to be deliberate with your energy and fuel for greatness.

Sometimes when I tapped my belly or played your favorite songs,
I could feel you dancing. Even though you couldn't see us yet,
we knew you could hear us, feel us, and laugh with us.

The better I took care of myself, the better I could take care of you. Self-care is not selfish.

All our naps, meditations, and workouts prepared me for
the big day when we would finally get to meet you.

But still, our sweat breaks were my favorite. I could feel you growing stronger. And we were already making memories.

Your favorite activities involved lacing up, lifting heavy, and getting sweaty! With every mile, repetition, and drop of sweat, I could feel your energy growing. Endorphins were our magic.

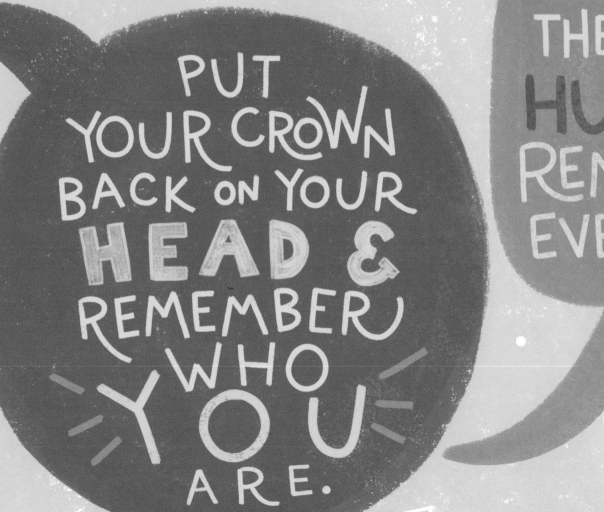

After nine months of excitement, we were ready to meet you.

All our training prepared us for this special day. It would be our biggest workout yet.

The moment you arrived, our lives changed. I'm grateful that your soul chose mine. You complete our family.

We are stronger together.

Abuela couldn't wait to hold you. She proclaimed, "¡Aquí está Pequeño! ¡Celebremos!" Pequeño is here! Let's celebrate!

This is your reminder that our hustle and bond started from our first workout together. We will always be a dream team. I will be here to encourage you, and you'll inspire me in return.

Together we have the courage to adventure, to feel, to see, to accept, to heal, to be.

Welcome to the world, baby. The next chapter of this story is yours to write now. We'll all keep cheering you on along your journey.

FOR CARMEN AMELIA, THE ORIGINAL SUPERHERO —RA

TO ALL CAREGIVERS WHO FILL THEIR COMMUNITIES
WITH LOVE AND KINDNESS —ARS